ANIMAL BABIES

BABY RED PANDAS

by Jennifer Boothroyd

Consultant: Beth Gambro
Reading Specialist, Yorkville, Illinois

BEARPORT PUBLISHING

Minneapolis, Minnesota

Teaching Tips

Before Reading

- Look at the cover of the book. Discuss the picture and the title.
- Ask readers to brainstorm a list of what they already know about red pandas. What can they expect to see in this book?
- Go on a picture walk, looking through the pictures to discuss vocabulary and make predictions about the text.

During Reading

- Read for purpose. Encourage readers to think about red pandas and the animal life cycle as they are reading.
- If readers encounter an unknown word, ask them to look at the sounds in the word. Then, ask them to look at the rest of the page. Are there any clues to help them understand?

After Reading

- Encourage readers to pick a buddy and reread the book together.
- Ask readers to name three things that red pandas do between the time they are born and when they are ready to have babies. Go back and find the pages that tell about these things.
- Ask readers to write a sentence and draw a picture of something that they learned about red pandas.

Credits:
Cover and title page, © CTK/Alamy Stock Photo; 3, © Eric Isselee/Shutterstock; 5, © UPI/Alamy Stock Photo; 7, © ODD ANDERSEN/Getty Images; 9, © UPI/Alamy Stock Photo; 11, © Olga Bogatyrenko/Dreamstime; 12, © Cuson/Shutterstock; 15, © moranaF/iStock; 16, © AB Photographie/Shutterstock; 18-19, © Jose Angel Astor Rocha/Shutterstock; 20, © Lukas Blazek/Dreamstime; 22, © Tao Jiang/Shutterstock; 23BL, © Axel Gebauer/Minden Pictures; 23BR, © UPI/Alamy Stock Photo; 23TL, © hudiemm/iStock; 23TR, © Blanka Berankova/Shutterstock

Library of Congress Cataloging-in-Publication Data

Names: Boothroyd, Jennifer, 1972- author.
Title: Baby red pandas / Jennifer Boothroyd.
Description: Bearcub books edition. | Minneapolis, Minnesota : Bearport
Publishing Company, [2021] | Series: Animal babies | Includes bibliographical references and index.
Identifiers: LCCN 2020038307 (print) | LCCN 2020038308 (ebook) | ISBN
9781647474720 (library binding) | ISBN 9781647474805 (paperback) | ISBN
9781647474881 (ebook)
Subjects: LCSH: Red panda—Infancy—Juvenile literature.
Classification: LCC QL737.C214 B64 2021 (print) | LCC QL737 .C214 (ebook)
| DDC 599.76/3—dc23
LC record available at https://lccn.loc.gov/2020038307
LC ebook record available at https://lccn.loc.gov/2020038308

For more information, write to Bearport Publishing, 5357 Penn Avenue South, Minneapolis, MN 55419.

Printed in the United States of America.

Contents

It's a Baby Red Panda!

A red panda mother is red.

But her baby is not.

The little panda has gray fur.

A red panda baby is called a **cub**.

It is the size of your hand.

The **newborn** cub cannot open its eyes.

It does not hear yet.

Eee!

The baby is hungry.

It drinks milk from its mother's body.

Then, it sleeps.

In a few weeks, the cub opens its eyes.

It can see and hear.

It starts to grow red fur, too.

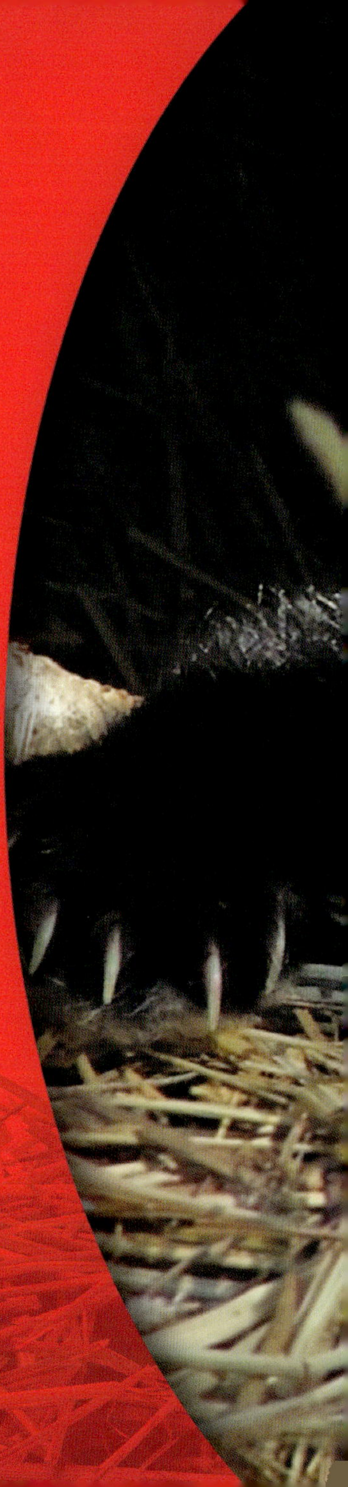

The cub grows bigger.

Soon, its mother brings it **bamboo**.

The little red panda has a taste.

But it still mostly drinks milk.

When the cub is three months old, it leaves the **den**.

The little red panda starts to climb trees.

It learns to find bamboo to eat.

Now the cub looks more like its mother.

It has red and white fur on its face.

Its legs are covered in black fur.

In two months, it stops drinking milk.

It eats mostly bamboo and other plants.

The cub is fully grown.

When the red panda is a year old, its mother leaves.

The young red panda is on its own.

In six more months, it can start to have cubs.

The Baby's Body

Glossary

bamboo a plant with leaves and a thick stem

cub a baby animal, such as a red panda

den an animal home

newborn a baby that was just born

Index

Read More

Borgert-Spaniol, Megan. *Red Pandas (Blastoff! Readers: Animal Safari).* Minneapolis: Bellwether Media, 2016.

Rudolph, Jessica. *My Whiskers Are Long and White (Zoo Clues 2).* New York: Bearport Publishing, 2017.

Learn More Online

1. Go to **www.factsurfer.com**
2. Enter "**Baby Red Pandas**" into the search box.
3. Click on the cover of this book to see a list of websites.

About the Author

Jennifer Boothroyd enjoys visiting museums and nature centers.